I0821666

MICHIGAN STATE SPARTANS

BY TODD KARPOVICH

SportsZone

An Imprint of Abdo Publishing
abdopublishing.com

abdopublishing.com

Published by Abdo Publishing, a division of ABDO, PO Box 398166, Minneapolis, Minnesota 55439.

Printed in the United States of America, North Mankato, Minnesota
042018
092018

Cover Photo: Andrew Nelles/AP Images
Interior Photos: Andrew Nelles/AP Images, 1; AP Images, 4–5, 8, 12–13, 17, 21, 42 (top), 43 (top left); Michigan State/Collegiate Images/Getty Images, 7, 42 (bottom left); Bettmann/Getty Images, 11, 33; Michigan History Magazine/The Oakland Press/AP Images, 15; Joseph Scherschel/The LIFE Picture Collection/Getty Images, 18–19, 43 (top right); Preston Stroup/AP Images, 22; Mark Kauffman/The LIFE Picture Collection/Getty Images, 25; Bettmann/Corbis/Getty Images, 26–27; James Drake/Sports Illustrated/Getty Images, 30–31; Al Goldis/AP Images, 35, 39; Collegiate Images/Getty Images, 36–37; Brandon Wade/AP Images, 40, 43 (bottom); David E. Klutho/Sports Illustrated/Getty Images, 42 (bottom right); Brad Schloss/AP Images, 44

Editor: Julie Dick
Series Designer: Craig Hinton

Library of Congress Control Number: 2017962090

Publisher's Cataloging-in-Publication Data

Names: Karpovich, Todd, author.
Title: Michigan State Spartans / by Todd Karpovich.
Description: Minneapolis, Minnesota : Abdo Publishing, 2019. | Series: Inside college football | Includes online resources and index.
Identifiers: ISBN 9781532114588 (lib.bdg.) | ISBN 9781532154416 (ebook)
Subjects: LCSH: American football--Juvenile literature. | College sports--United States--History--Juvenile literature. | Michigan State University. Spartans (Football team)--Juvenile literature. | Football--Records--United States--Juvenile literature.
Classification: DDC 796.332630--dc23

TABLE OF CONTENTS

Fans filled Spartan Stadium for the 1966 Michigan State-Notre Dame game.

"THE GAME OF THE CENTURY"

MICHIGAN STATE UNIVERSITY SENIOR BUBBA SMITH WAS IN HIS DORM ROOM ON A CRISP FALL NIGHT IN 1966. A FAMILIAR CHANT AROSE FROM OUTSIDE HIS WINDOW. A CROWD OF APPROXIMATELY 5,000 STUDENTS HAD GATHERED OUTSIDE ON THE LAWN. THEY WERE CHANTING "KILL, BUBBA, KILL!" THAT CHEER WAS USUALLY RESERVED FOR SATURDAY AFTERNOONS. THAT'S WHEN SMITH, A 6-FOOT-6-INCH, 280-POUND DEFENSIVE END, USUALLY SPENT HIS DAY TERRORIZING OPPOSING QUARTERBACKS.

But this was a special week. On November 19, 1966, second-ranked Michigan State would play No. 1 Notre Dame. Fans and media began calling it "The Game of the Century."

The rivalry between the Spartans and the Fighting Irish dated to 1897. Now they were about to meet as the two highest-ranked teams in the country. The Spartans had already won five national titles. But the Fighting Irish were ranked No. 1 for good reason. They had outscored their opponents by a whopping 301–28 in winning their first eight games of the season.

Michigan State boasted a talented roster. Its bone-crunching defense was led by Smith and defensive back George Webster. The Spartans entered the game 9–0 on the season and had won their previous 19 regular-season games.

The Notre Dame defensive line featured All-Americans Alan Page, Pete Duranko, and Kevin Hardy. Linebacker Jim Lynch won the Maxwell Award that season as the nation's best college football player. The game featured 25 All-Americans and eight future first-round draft picks in the National Football League (NFL).

A REAL CROWD-PLEASER

The United States had troops overseas fighting in the Vietnam War (1954–1975). Military leaders tried to make them feel at home as much as possible. One way to do that was by helping them keep in touch with the sports world back in the United States. And the troops couldn't miss "The Game of the Century." So the Michigan State-Notre Dame game broadcast overseas to US troops.

People at home were clamoring to see it, too. ABC-TV received approximately 50,000 letters and petitions to air the game. The network decided to cover what was essentially the 1966 national championship game. That proved to be a wise move. The game drew a national television audience of more than 30 million viewers. That would be a huge number even by today's standards. "The Game of the Century" even attracted more viewers than the first Super Bowl, which was played two months later in Los Angeles.

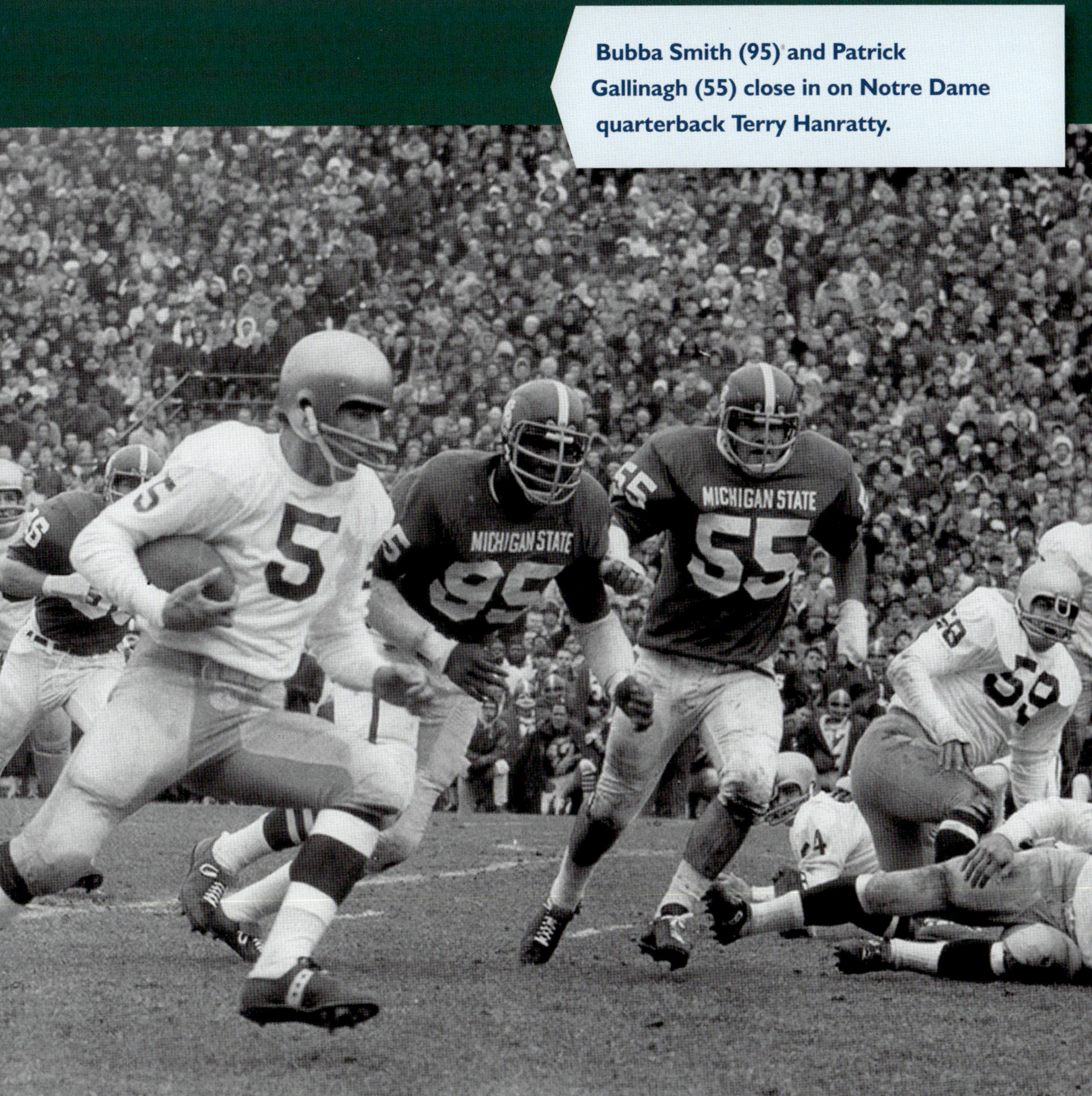

Bubba Smith (95) and Patrick Gallinagh (55) close in on Notre Dame quarterback Terry Hanratty.

On game day, more than 80,000 fans packed Spartan Stadium. Millions more watched on television. Notre Dame won the coin toss and elected to open the game on offense. But the Michigan State defense would set the early tone.

Notre Dame coach Ara Parseghian, *left*, shakes hands with Michigan State coach Duffy Daugherty after the game.

A big hit by Smith knocked Notre Dame quarterback Terry Hanratty out of the game in the opening quarter. Hanratty was one of Notre Dame's All-Americans. *Sports Illustrated* and *Time* had both featured him on their covers. He suffered a separated shoulder on Smith's hit and was done for the day. On that same play, Irish guard George Goeddeke sprained an ankle. The Spartans gained a huge advantage with two key Notre Dame players out of the lineup.

The Spartans took a 10–0 lead on a 5-yard touchdown run by Regis Cavender and a field goal by Dick Kenney. But Notre Dame fought back with sophomore Coley O'Brien replacing Hanratty as quarterback. Midway through the second quarter, O'Brien threw a 34-yard touchdown pass to Bob Gladieux. That brought the score to 10–7. Then Notre Dame kicker Joe Azzaro made a 42-yard field goal late in the third quarter to tie the game.

From there, neither team was able to find the end zone again. Notre Dame was criticized for its conservative approach in the fourth quarter. The Irish knew that a tie would likely keep them ahead of the Spartans in the national polls. So with Notre Dame playing it safe, "The Game of the Century" ended in a 10–10 tie.

Media outlets disagreed over who had played better. Michigan State was ranked No. 1 in the coaches poll, but Notre Dame earned the top ranking in the Associated Press media poll. Each team finished the season 9–0–1 and claimed a share of the national championship.

QUOTABLE

"We'd fought hard to come back and tie it up. After all that, I didn't want to risk giving it to them cheap."
—Notre Dame head coach Ara Parseghian defending his decision to settle for the tie

Michigan State also won its second straight Big Ten Conference title. However, due to rules that have since changed, the Spartans didn't go to a bowl game. The Big Ten had an agreement in place to send its champion to the Rose Bowl each year. But at the time, the conference didn't allow teams to go in consecutive years.

MR. HOLLYWOOD

Defensive end Bubba Smith won a Super Bowl with the Baltimore Colts in 1970. He also was named first-team All-Pro in 1971. After Smith retired from football, he became a popular actor, appearing in the *Police Academy* films.

Because Michigan State had played in the Rose Bowl the year before, second-place Purdue went in its place. And because the Big Ten didn't let its teams play in any other bowls, the Spartans stayed home for the holidays.

Meanwhile, the rivalry between Michigan State and Notre Dame endures today. Although the Fighting Irish don't play in the Big Ten, the football teams still play each other on a regular basis. The winner of the Michigan State–Notre Dame game is awarded the Megaphone Trophy. The trophy was first awarded in 1949. It is shaped like a megaphone and lists game scores for each matchup. And in 2017 former Michigan State and Notre Dame players met for a "Game of the Century" reunion at Michigan State. It is believed to be the first time the men who played that game had gathered together since their matchup 51 years earlier.

Clinton Jones was a star running back for Michigan State from 1964 through 1966.

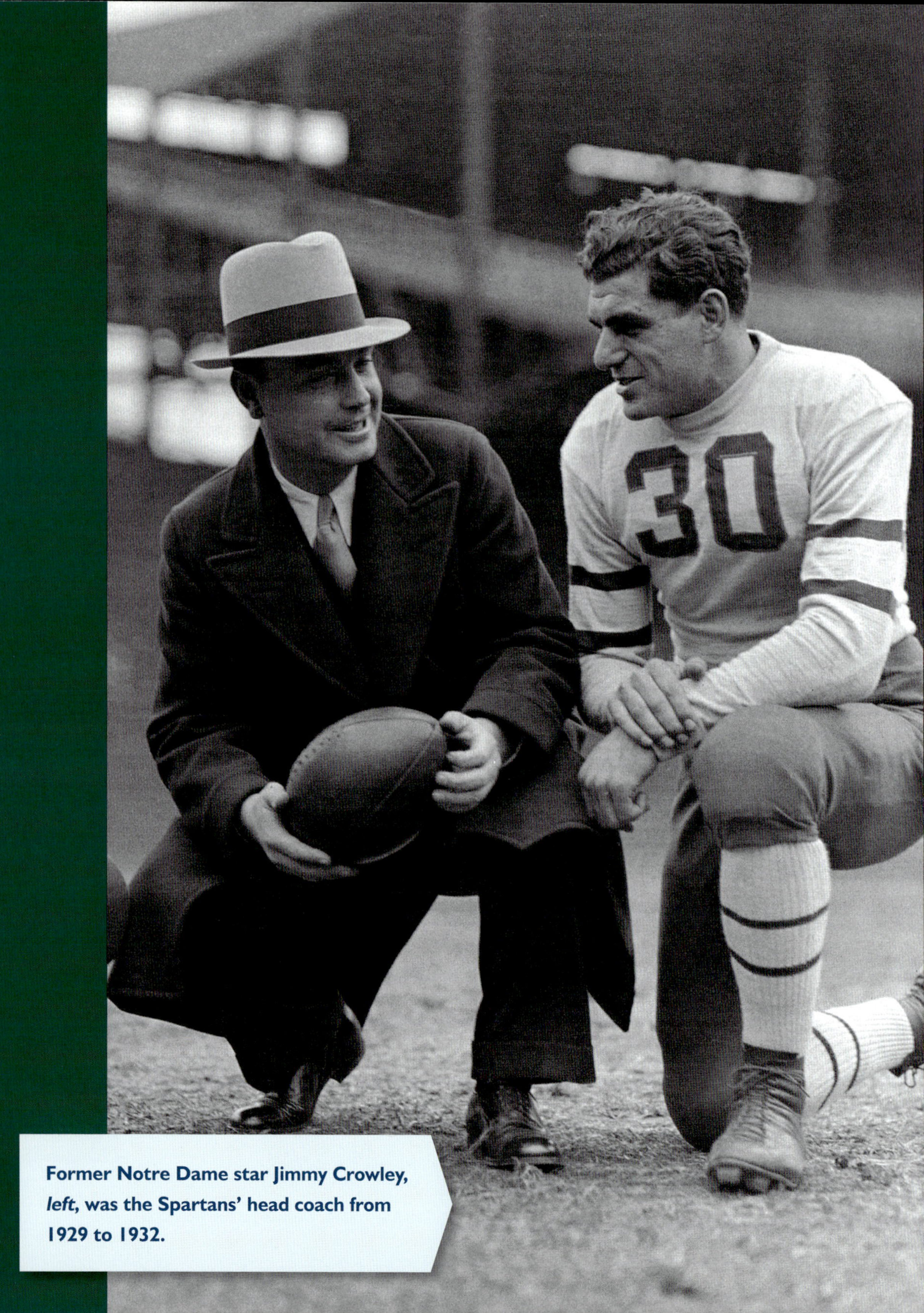

Former Notre Dame star Jimmy Crowley, *left*, was the Spartans' head coach from 1929 to 1932.

2

THE EARLY YEARS

THE MICHIGAN STATE FOOTBALL PROGRAM BEGAN IN 1896 ON THE CAMPUS AT EAST LANSING, MICHIGAN. BACK THEN THE SCHOOL WAS KNOWN AS MICHIGAN AGRICULTURAL COLLEGE. THE TEAM WAS NICKNAMED THE AGGIES. THEY PLAYED ONLY FOUR GAMES IN THEIR FIRST SEASON, DUE TO DIFFICULTIES WITH TRAVEL. THEY FINISHED 1–2–1. THEIR ONLY WIN WAS AGAINST LANSING HIGH SCHOOL.

In 1897 the team went 4–2–1 under head coach Henry Keep. The engineering student was given the job because of his success coaching the track team. Keep finished with a career record of 8–5–1.

Chester Brewer got the team on the right track when he took over the program in 1903. He was a former four-sport athlete at the University of Wisconsin. Brewer took over as the head coach in 1903 and stayed on through 1910. Then he became the school's first full-time athletic director. He came back to coach the football team in 1917 and 1919.

Under Brewer, the Aggies went 58–23–7 and never lost at home. The defense recorded 49 shutouts. Brewer also coached baseball and basketball. He was named to the Michigan State Athletics Hall of Fame. Today, the Chester L. Brewer Award is given annually to a graduating Michigan State senior for success in sports and academics. The scholarship also lists character, personality, and other leadership qualities as factors in determining its recipient.

John Macklin followed Brewer as coach. His teams went 29–5 from 1911 to 1915. Macklin's .853 career winning percentage remained second best in school history going into the 2018 season. Under Macklin, the Aggies enjoyed their first perfect season, going 7–0 in 1913. That was also the first year that a black player, Gideon Smith, joined the team. Smith was a star tackle for the Aggies. Jerry DaPrato and Blake Miller became the school's first All-Americans in 1915.

Macklin also led Michigan State to its first victories over Ohio State and Michigan. Both of those schools would become major rivals in the Big Ten Conference.

RIVAL WOLVERINES

Through the years, the Spartans have developed a spirited rivalry with their neighbors, the University of Michigan Wolverines. The teams play each year as members of the Big Ten. The winner takes home the Paul Bunyan–Governor of Michigan Trophy. Heading into the 2018 season, Michigan led the series 54–34–4. But Michigan State had won eight of the previous 10 meetings.

The Paul Bunyan-Governor of Michigan Trophy goes to the winner of the annual Michigan State-Michigan game.

In 1925 Michigan Agricultural College was officially renamed Michigan State College. The college held a contest to choose a new nickname. The winner was "The Michigan Staters." Sports editor George Alderton of the *Lansing State Journal* thought the name was too awkward. He decided to look through the other contest entries. Alderton found the nickname "Spartans" and went with that instead.

SPARTAN STADIUM

In 1923 the Spartans moved their games to the site of the current Spartan Stadium. At the time, the stadium could hold 14,000 people. The heated rivalry with Michigan often filled the stadium. But when Michigan hosted the game, more than 100,000 fans could attend, so Michigan State hosted the game only twice in 40 years. Supporters feared the game would be permanently hosted in Ann Arbor. An expansion in 1957 added a second deck to the east and west sides of the stadium. The seating capacity grew from 50,011 to 75,000. Fears of being forced to move home games to Ann Arbor were alleviated.

Former Notre Dame standout Jimmy Crowley became coach in 1929. He led the Spartans to winning seasons in his first four years. The Notre Dame influence continued when Crowley stepped down and fellow Fighting Irish alum Charles Bachman took over. Bachman continued the Spartans' revival with 10 winning seasons in the next 13 years.

Bachman led the program to its first bowl game. In 1937 the Spartans went 8–1. The only blemish on the regular-season record was a 3–0 loss at Manhattan College. The squad rebounded to win its final six games. The defense allowed only 19 points during that span.

The Spartans' reward was a trip to Miami, Florida, to play in a relatively new game called the Orange Bowl. It was only the fourth time the game was played. The Spartans lost to Auburn University 6–0 on January 1, 1938. Through 2017 it remained the only time a Michigan State team was invited to the Orange Bowl.

The Spartans (dark jerseys) played Auburn in the Orange Bowl on January 1, 1938.

Like many other schools around the country, Michigan State suspended its program in 1943 because of World War II (1939–1945). Many students left campus to help the Allied cause. When the war ended, Michigan State football was ready to take a giant leap forward onto the national stage.

Clarence "Biggie" Munn helped put the Spartans on the map when he took over as Michigan State's head coach.

3

BIG SUCCESS

FOR THE FIRST HALF OF THE 20TH CENTURY, THE MICHIGAN WOLVERINES WERE THE TEAM TO BEAT. THE BOYS FROM THE BIG SCHOOL IN ANN ARBOR HAD WON MULTIPLE ROSE BOWLS. THEY TRAVELED THROUGHOUT THE COUNTRY TO PLAY OTHER BIG-NAME PROGRAMS. THE WOLVERINES WERE ONE OF THE POWERS OF THE WESTERN CONFERENCE.

Michigan State, on the other hand, was mostly an afterthought. The Spartans didn't have a conference. They had to find opponents one year at a time.

That began to change when Clarence "Biggie" Munn took over as the Spartans' head coach in 1947. Munn had been an All-American guard at the University of Minnesota. He coached one year at Syracuse University. Then he was hired to turn things around at Michigan State. School president John Hannah was on a mission to raise the school's national profile. Hannah counted on Munn's football program to play a key role in that mission.

Munn's first game against Michigan showed him how difficult the task might be. The Wolverines outscored the Spartans 95–7 in the previous two games. The first game at Michigan Stadium went even worse. The Wolverines blasted the Spartans 55–0. The loss showed that Michigan State had a long way to go.

One way to judge Munn's progress is to look at results against Michigan. The gap began to close immediately. In 1948 the rivals met for the first time in East Lansing. Michigan pulled out a narrow 13–7 victory. The next year in Ann Arbor, the Wolverines won their 10th straight game against the Spartans. This time Michigan won by only a 7–3 margin.

The second game of the 1950 season offered Michigan State a chance at redemption. The Spartans had a solid season. Their season ended with a 6–3 record. That record earned them a No. 19 ranking in

BIGGIE'S WISDOM

Clarence "Biggie" Munn had plenty of success in his tenure at Michigan State. According to former Spartans offensive lineman Carl Nystrom, Munn's mental approach to the game resulted in stronger play on game day.

"He always had some kind of psychological effect that he would incorporate during the week," Nystrom said. "He had that rough, gruff voice and the two words that you learned from Biggie were 'demand and confront.' He would demand that you worked hard and performed well and all of those kind of good things. But if you didn't do it the right way, he'd confront you and get on your butt. You had a little scare in you when you played for him, but he had a good way of doing it. He didn't do it in a vicious way."

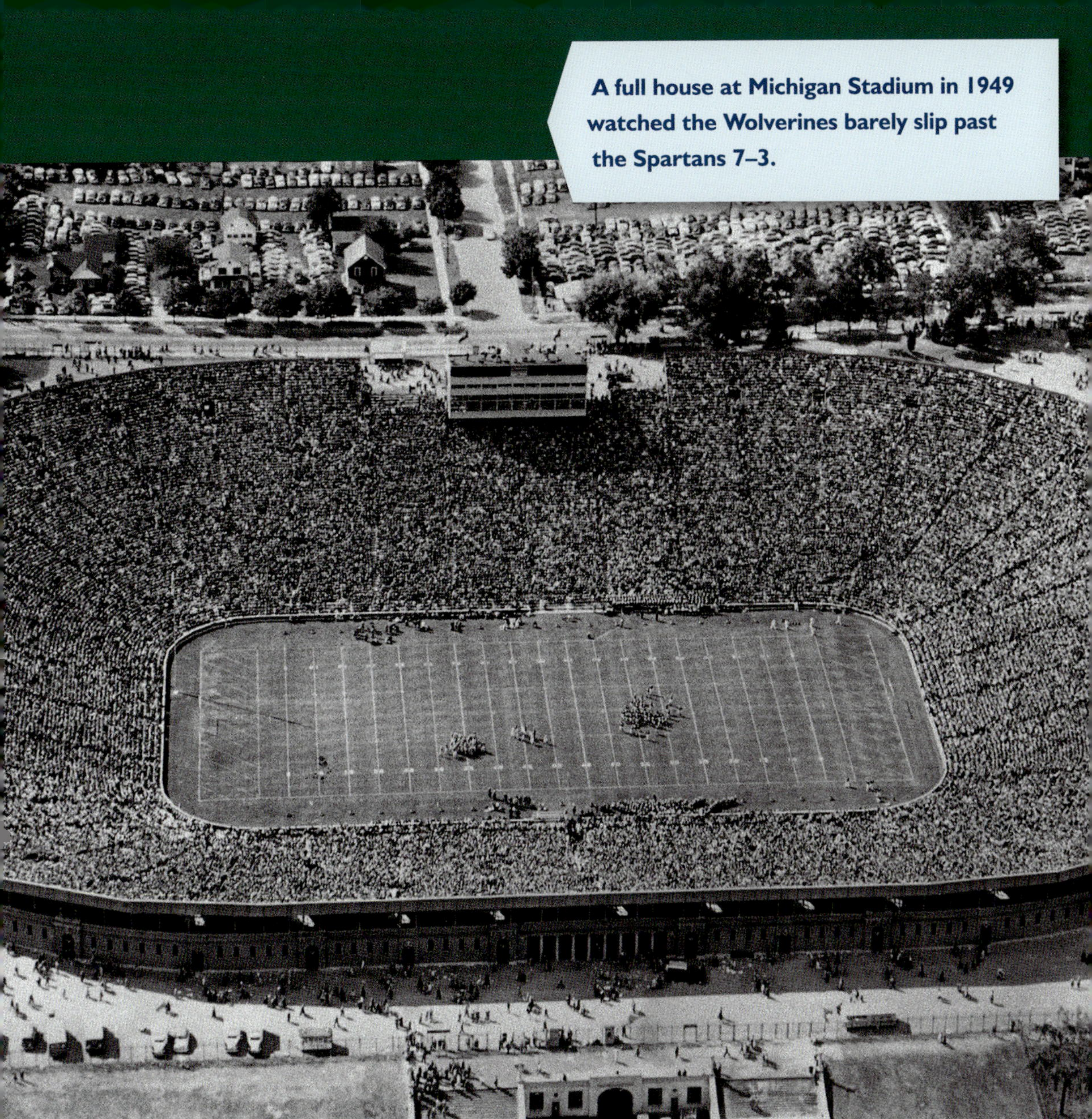

A full house at Michigan Stadium in 1949 watched the Wolverines barely slip past the Spartans 7–3.

the final national poll. The Spartans won a season-opening victory over Oregon State. The Spartans headed to Ann Arbor to face the No. 3 Wolverines. Tied in the fourth quarter, Spartans fullback Leroy Crane scored the go-ahead touchdown. A late interception sealed the 14–7 victory for Michigan State.

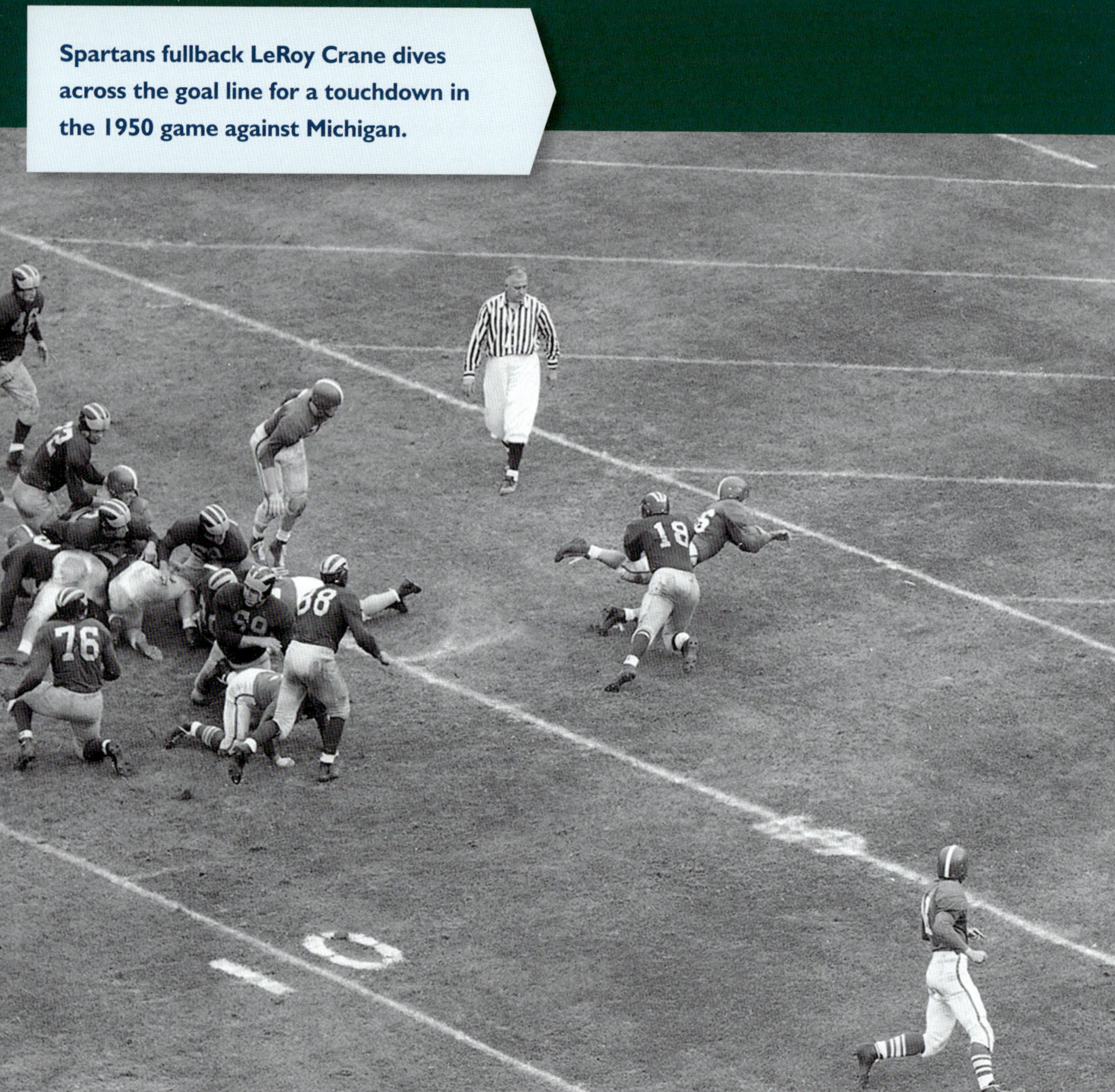

Spartans fullback LeRoy Crane dives across the goal line for a touchdown in the 1950 game against Michigan.

That victory vaulted the Spartans to the No. 2 ranking in the next national poll. That turned out to be short-lived as Maryland came to East Lansing and drilled the Spartans 34–7 the next week. But that was the only blemish on the 1950 season. A season-ending six-game winning streak pushed Michigan State all the way to No. 8 in the national poll.

That set the stage for a remarkable two-season run that few teams have ever matched. In 1951 the Spartans opened the year ranked No. 2 in the country before posting early road wins over Michigan and Ohio State. They also won at Penn State and beat No. 11 Notre Dame at home en route to a perfect 9–0 record. One national poll put Michigan State at the head of the pack. But the Associated Press and other organizations gave the nod to 10–0 Tennessee. Tennessee went on to lose to Maryland in the Sugar Bowl.

HALL OF FAMERS

Nine of Michigan State's most outstanding former players have been inducted into the College Football Hall of Fame.

- halfback John Pingel (1968)
- tackle Don Coleman (1975)
- linebacker George Webster (1987)
- defensive end Bubba Smith (1988)
- safety Brad Van Pelt (2001)
- wide receiver Gene Washington (2011)
- linebacker Percy Snow (2013)
- running back Clinton Jones (2015)
- wide receiver Kirk Gibson (2017)

Four other members of the College Football Hall of Fame are former Spartans head coaches.

- Clarence "Biggie" Munn (1959)
- Charles W. Bachman (1978)
- Duffy Daugherty (1984)
- Frank "Muddy" Waters (2000)

Michigan State opened the 1952 season ranked No. 1 in the nation. That's pretty much where it stayed the rest of the year. A slight bobble in the form of a 17–14 road victory against a weak Oregon State team pushed the Spartans back to No. 2 for a week. But they pounded Texas A&M 48–6 in their next game and jumped right back to No. 1. From there, the Spartans ran the table. Victories over No. 17 Penn State, No. 8 Purdue, and No. 6 Notre Dame showed that they were capable of beating the best of the best. And at the end of the year, all 11 polls showed Michigan State at the top. The "little brother" of Michigan football was the consensus national champion.

That title set the stage for another leap forward for the program. The Spartans were about to join one of college football's most exclusive clubs.

POLL POLITICS

The National Collegiate Athletic Association (NCAA) used to decide its Division I national championship on paper, not on the gridiron. Media organizations and coaching associations once conducted polls of their members to determine the national champion.

In some years, the NCAA recognized more than a dozen national polls. Teams that were ranked No. 1 in all of the recognized polls were considered "consensus champions." But that didn't happen often. In most years, multiple teams claimed a share of the national championship, leading to what was known as a "split championship." In 1992 the NCAA began taking steps to ensure that the No. 1 and No. 2 teams would face off in a bowl game to determine the national title on the field. Today, the College Football Playoff committee ranks the top four teams in the nation, who face off in two national semifinals. The semifinal winners square off in the national championship game.

Michigan State defenders put up a fight against a Notre Dame ball carrier in 1952.

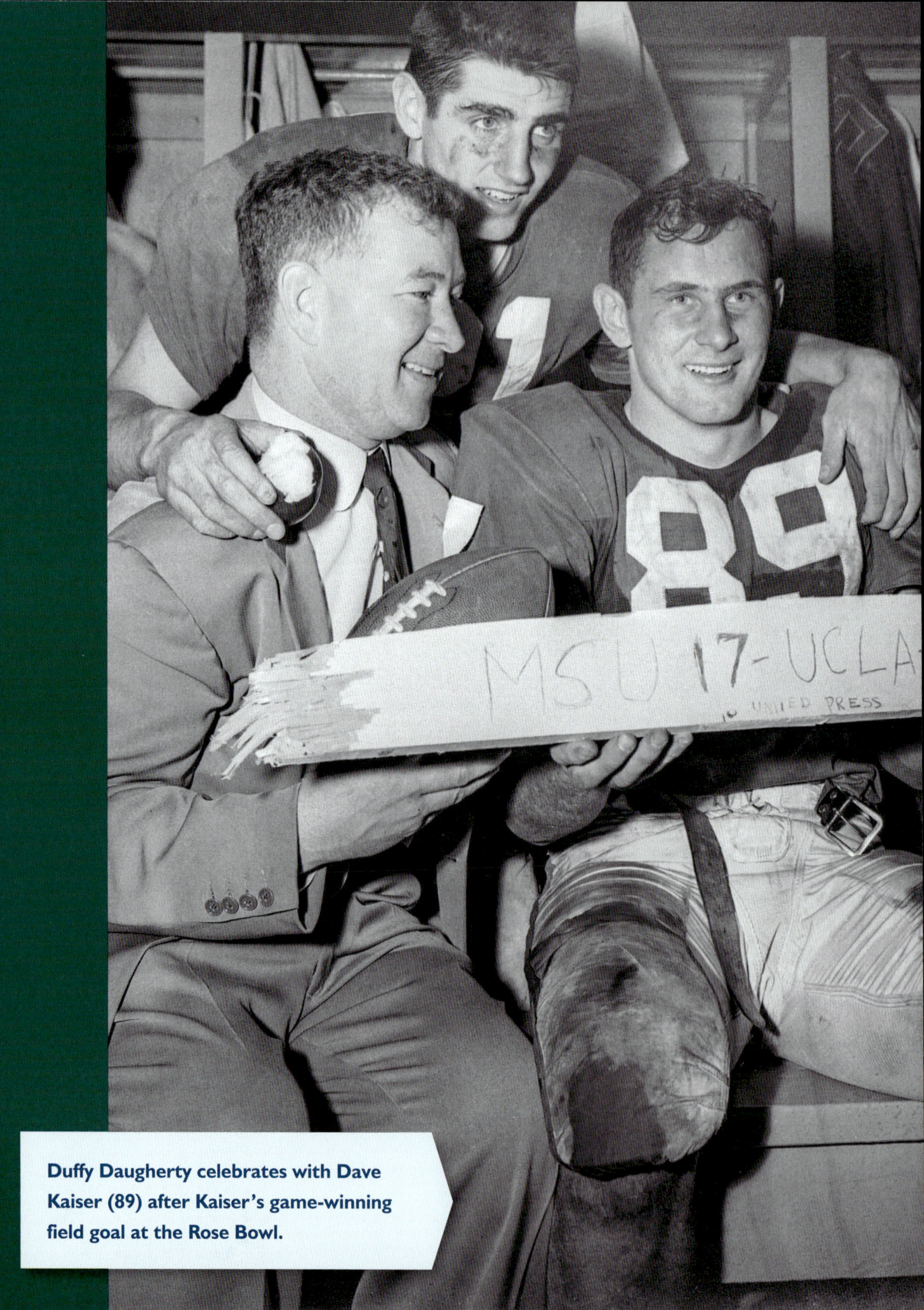

Duffy Daugherty celebrates with Dave Kaiser (89) after Kaiser's game-winning field goal at the Rose Bowl.

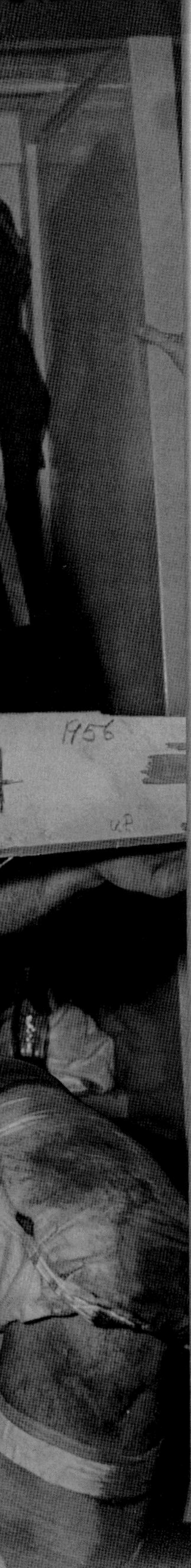

BIG TEN, BIG SPLASH

AFTER POSTING BACK-TO-BACK 9–0 SEASONS, THE MICHIGAN STATE SPARTANS WERE ONE OF THE MOST SUCCESSFUL AND RESPECTED PROGRAMS IN THE COUNTRY. AND IN 1953, THEY JOINED ONE OF THE MOST SUCCESSFUL AND RESPECTED CONFERENCES IN THE COUNTRY.

The Western Conference—unofficially called the Big Ten, referring to the number of schools in the conference since 1917—lost a member immediately after World War II. The University of Chicago had minimized sports during the war. Then it dropped out in 1946, citing an inability to compete with the other nine schools.

Michigan State immediately began to lobby to replace Chicago in the conference. However, its bid faced strong resistance from the University of Michigan. The Wolverines didn't want to legitimize their rival and hurt their own recruiting. Other schools fought Michigan State's admission for other reasons. But in the end, the Spartans were chosen to make the Big Ten whole again.

Though officially admitted for the 1949–50 season, the Spartans weren't allowed to join for football until the schedules already drawn up had been played. That meant independent status for Munn's team for three more seasons. But in 1953, the new era of Big Ten football was launched with defending national champion Michigan State joining the fray.

DON COLEMAN

Offensive linemen generally get little fanfare. But tackle Don Coleman is widely regarded as having a huge impact on the program. In 1951 he became the first black football player in Michigan State history to be named an All-American. He also came in second for the Outland Trophy, given to the nation's top lineman.

It was another banner year for the Spartans. They started the season ranked No. 2 in the nation. They kicked off Big Ten play with a 21–7 victory at Iowa and were 4–0 when they played at Purdue. Their 28-game winning streak came to a crashing halt in a 6–0 loss. But the Spartans rebounded to win their final four regular-season games. They claimed a share of the Big Ten title in their first year in the conference. Then they represented the Big Ten in the Rose Bowl. A 28–20 win over the University of California, Los Angeles (UCLA) capped another great season in East Lansing.

Munn retired after that season but stayed on as Michigan State's athletic director. He was succeeded by Duffy Daugherty, who maintained his predecessor's success. In 1955 Michigan State was back on the top of the college football world. The Spartans went 9–1. Their only loss came to No. 2 Michigan in a 14-7 thriller at Ann Arbor. They went on to win their final eight games to end the season ranked No. 2 in the nation.

Michigan State again faced UCLA in the Rose Bowl. In the final seconds, Spartans kicker Dave Kaiser made a 41-yard field goal. That gave the Spartans a 17–14 victory over the fourth-ranked Bruins.

In 1957 Michigan State claimed a share of its fourth national title of the decade. The Spartans finished 8–1 and outscored their opponents 264–75. However, a 20–13 loss to Purdue cost them a perfect season and the Big Ten spot in the Rose Bowl.

KICKING CONFUSION

Dave Kaiser was a surprise choice for the game-winning field goal in the Rose Bowl victory over UCLA. The Spartans used two players for placekicks, as they were called in those days. Jerry Planutis kicked extra points and short field goals. Kaiser was the man for longer field goal attempts. But Kaiser injured his leg early in the season and hadn't attempted a field goal since.

Earlier in the Rose Bowl, Planutis had made two extra-point kicks. But he'd also missed two field goals. When it came time to make the call, Spartans coach Duffy Daugherty went with Kaiser for the 41-yard try.

Amazingly, Kaiser had lost one of his contact lenses and couldn't see the uprights clearly. And the Spartans center snapped the ball early, catching Kaiser in the middle of a practice kick. But he stepped back and quickly swung his leg again. But he couldn't bear to watch. He turned away from the uprights, learning only from the referee's call that his kick was good.

Bubba Smith wraps up Notre Dame running back Larry Conjar in 1966.

CHAMPIONS AGAIN

MICHIGAN STATE'S NEXT TURN IN THE NATIONAL SPOTLIGHT ARRIVED IN 1965. THE SPARTANS WERE LOADED WITH TALENT. FIVE PLAYERS WERE HONORED AS ALL-AMERICANS. THEY WERE FULLBACK BOB APISA, HALFBACK CLINTON JONES, WIDE RECEIVER GENE WASHINGTON, DEFENSIVE END BUBBA SMITH, AND LINEBACKER GEORGE WEBSTER. THE SPARTANS' DEFENSE WAS NICKNAMED THE "WALL OF STEEL." IT ALLOWED JUST 6.9 POINTS PER GAME, THE THIRD-FEWEST IN THE NATION.

The defense came through in the Spartans' two toughest games. A 14–10 victory at No. 6 Purdue on October 23 vaulted Michigan State to the top spot in the national rankings. And a 12–3 win at Notre Dame closed out a 10–0 regular season.

However, UCLA earned a measure of revenge, beating Michigan State 14–12 in the Rose Bowl. Still, the Spartans were impressive enough for some voters to rank them as national champions for a fifth time.

GEORGE WEBSTER

George Webster, who played for Michigan State from 1964 to 1966, was a defensive dynamo. He could line up at safety, linebacker, or defensive end. That created headaches for the offense. At 6 feet 4 inches tall and 218 pounds, Webster punished opponents who tried to make a play on his side of the field. He was a two-time All-American as he led the Spartans to two Big Ten titles and national championship honors. As a senior he made 93 tackles, including 10 for loss. He was named the team Most Valuable Player (MVP) that year.

Webster was regarded as one of the best players in Spartans' football history. His legacy lives on in academics as well. In February 2007, Michigan State established the George Webster Scholarship Fund. The scholarship is given to two former student-athletes each year so they can return and complete their degrees. Webster was a proponent of athletes using their education after their playing days.

The Spartans did it again the next year. The highlight of the 1966 season was the 10–10 tie with Notre Dame in "The Game of the Century." The Spartans finished the year 9–0–1. Michigan State was crowned national champion by the Football Research poll. Another poll conducted by the Helms Foundation named them co-champions. That team also had four players chosen in the top eight selections of the NFL Draft: Smith, Jones, Webster, and Washington.

The 1970s were not great years for Spartans football. However, the decade did feature one of the most memorable games ever played at Spartan Stadium. On November 9, 1974, Michigan State knocked off top-ranked Ohio State 16–13. The Spartans trailed 13–9 with less than

Michigan State's 1965 defensive line: *from left,* Bob Viney, Don Bierow, Harold Lucas, Buddy Owens, and Bubba Smith

four minutes remaining in the game. Then Michigan State running back Levi Jackson ran 88 yards for the go-ahead touchdown. But Ohio State wasn't done. The Buckeyes drove all the way to the Spartans 1-yard line in the final seconds. However, the Spartans rallied to stuff Ohio State fullback Champ Henson at the goal line on the game's last play. It is

MAGIC MOMENT

In 2013 Michigan State played its 500th game at Spartan Stadium. To celebrate, fans were polled on their favorite game. The 2011 game against Wisconsin got the most votes.

In that game, the score was tied 31–31 with time running out in the fourth quarter. Overtime appeared to be certain. But the Spartans had one last chance from the Wisconsin 44-yard line. Quarterback Kirk Cousins rolled to his right and launched the ball high in the air down the right sideline. The ball was batted out of the end zone, but Spartans receiver Keith Nichol caught the deflection at the 1-yard line.

Nichol kept his balance and forced his way toward the goal line. Three Badgers tried to wrestle him back. The stadium went silent as the officials reviewed a video replay. The officials said the ball did cross the goal line while in Nichol's possession. The touchdown gave the Spartans a 37–31 victory.

still considered one of the greatest victories in program history.

One of the most decorated athletes to set foot on the Michigan State campus in the 1970s was wide receiver Kirk Gibson. However, he didn't go on to glory in the NFL. He became a Major League Baseball (MLB) star instead.

Gibson was named a first-team football All-American in 1978. He had 42 catches for 806 yards and seven touchdowns that season. During his career at Michigan State, Gibson caught 112 passes for 2,347 yards and 24 touchdowns. And he ranks first in school history with 21.0 yards per catch.

However, Gibson was also an excellent baseball player. He didn't play at Michigan State until his junior year. In his only college season, Gibson batted .390 and set a school record with 16 home runs. The Detroit Tigers selected him in the first round

Keith Nichol fights through two Wisconsin defenders to score the winning touchdown on October 22, 2011.

of the 1978 MLB draft. He went on to have a storied career. He is most famous for hitting a game-winning, pinch-hit home run in the 1988 World Series. Former MLB All-Star first baseman Steve Garvey also played both football and baseball at Michigan State. Garvey was a defensive back on the 1967 squad. He hit a grand slam in his first at-bat as a Spartan.

Andre Rison was a high-flying wide receiver for the Spartans in the late 1980s.

MODERN SPARTANS

AFTER SOME PEAKS AND VALLEYS WITH THE PROGRAM, MICHIGAN STATE ROSE AGAIN WITH THE ARRIVAL OF COACH GEORGE PERLES IN 1983. PERLES HAD WON FOUR SUPER BOWL CHAMPIONSHIPS AS AN ASSISTANT COACH WITH THE NFL'S PITTSBURGH STEELERS. HE BROUGHT THAT WINNING ATTITUDE WITH HIM TO MICHIGAN STATE. IN HIS SECOND YEAR, THE SPARTANS PLAYED ARMY IN THE CHERRY BOWL. IT WAS THEIR FIRST BOWL APPEARANCE SINCE THEY PLAYED IN THE ROSE BOWL ON JANUARY 1, 1966.

In 12 seasons under Perles, Michigan State played in seven bowl games and won one Big Ten title. In 1987 the Spartans went 9–2–1. Their only losses were against Notre Dame and Florida State, both nonconference foes ranked in the top 10. After rolling through the Big Ten schedule, Michigan State beat University of Southern California (USC) 20–17 in the Rose Bowl. Safety John Miller had two interceptions. The Spartans shut down USC's playmaking

A HOCKEY RECORD

Spartan Stadium was the site of a world record that was set on October 6, 2001. Michigan State's men's hockey team hosted archrival Michigan for an outdoor game at the football stadium. A record crowd of 74,554 were in attendance. At the time, it was the largest crowd ever at an outdoor hockey game.

quarterback, Rodney Peete, who lost a fourth-quarter fumble that ended a potential scoring drive. The Spartans finished the season ranked No. 8 in the nation.

From 1984 to 1987, the offense relied heavily on Lorenzo White, the Spartans' top running back. White finished his career with a school record 4,887 rushing yards. As a sophomore, he ran for 2,066 yards, also a Michigan State record. In his senior year, White was truly a workhorse for the Spartans. In a win over Indiana that clinched the Big Ten title, White carried the ball 56 times for 292 yards. The two-time All-American was taken by the Houston Oilers in the first round of the 1988 NFL Draft.

Andre Rison was another big-game player for Michigan State from 1985 to 1988. The speedy wide receiver finished atop the Spartans' career list with 146 catches and 2,992 receiving yards. Rison was an All-American as a senior. He was a first-round pick by the Indianapolis Colts in the 1989 NFL Draft. In 2017 Rison's son Hunter made his debut with the Spartans. He caught 19 passes as a freshman wide receiver.

Nick Saban is best known for coaching the University of Alabama. However, he also had a successful career at Michigan State. He served as Perles's defensive coordinator from 1983 to 1987. Saban returned

Michigan State and Michigan drew a record-breaking crowd for an outdoor hockey game at Spartan Stadium in 2001.

to East Lansing to take over as Michigan State's head coach in 1995. In the next five years, he led Michigan State to a 34–24–1 record. He was the first coach in school history to reach a bowl game in each of his first three seasons. Michigan State went to the Independence Bowl in 1995, the Sun Bowl in 1996, and the Aloha Bowl in 1997.

In 1999 the Spartans were ranked No. 7 in the national polls and tied for second place in the Big Ten. That year Michigan State defeated Notre Dame, Michigan, Ohio State, and Penn State in the same year for the first time since 1965. Saban was hired away by Louisiana State at the end of the regular season. Assistant coach Bobby Williams took over and led the Spartans to a victory over Florida in the Citrus Bowl.

The Spartans made just enough plays on defense to beat Baylor in a Cotton Bowl shootout.

The Spartans scuffled for a few years after Saban left, but in that time the program produced one of its finest wide receivers ever in Charles Rogers. He became the first Michigan State player to win the Biletnikoff Award as the nation's top receiver. In 2002 Rogers was named a consensus All-American even though the team finished just 4–8.

Head coach Mark Dantonio ushered in a new era for Michigan State football when he took over in 2007. Dantonio was in charge of turning things around after three straight losing seasons. He had almost immediate success. Dantonio led the Spartans to bowl games in each of his first nine years as coach. In 2014 he guided Michigan State to its first Rose Bowl victory in 26 years. The Spartans defeated Stanford 24–20 to finish the season 13–1. They were ranked No. 3 in the national polls.

The next two years, Dantonio and the Spartans found themselves in the Cotton Bowl. They beat No. 4 Baylor 42–41 on January 1, 2015. The next year the Cotton Bowl was also a semifinal for the College Football Playoff system. The Spartans were seeded third after a 12–1 regular season and their second Big Ten title in three years. But former Michigan State coach Saban and his second-ranked Alabama team beat the Spartans 38–0.

RECORD-SETTING RECEIVERS

Andre Rison caught nine passes for a school-record 252 yards and three touchdowns in a 34–27 loss to Georgia in the 1989 Gator Bowl. Eleven years later, Spartans receiver Plaxico Burress broke that record with 255 receiving yards against Michigan.

Dantonio got help from plenty of outstanding players along the way. Running back Le'Veon Bell ran for 3,346 yards and 33 touchdowns in 40 career games at Michigan State. He also rushed for 100 yards in a game 12 times.

Darqueze Dennard is the only Michigan State player to win the Jim Thorpe Award as the nation's best defensive back. He was also a unanimous All-American as a senior in 2013 and a two-time first-team All-Big Ten selection and helped the Spartans to the Rose Bowl. The Cincinnati Bengals selected him in the first round of the 2014 NFL Draft.

After a down season in 2016, the Spartans bounced back to go 10–3 in 2017. They capped the season with a 42–17 rout of Washington State in the Holiday Bowl, re-establishing themselves as one of the premier programs in the Big Ten.

1896
Michigan State, then known as Michigan Agricultural College, launches varsity football.

1908
The Aggies post their first undefeated season, going 6–0–2.

1923
The first game is played on the future site of Spartan Stadium.

1925
Michigan Agricultural College is renamed Michigan State College.

1926
Athletic teams become known as the Spartans.

1966
The November 19 game against Notre Dame game ends 10–10. It is later known as "The Game of the Century."

1974
The Spartans upset No. 1 Ohio State on November 9.

1983
George Perles becomes coach. He leads the team to seven bowl games.

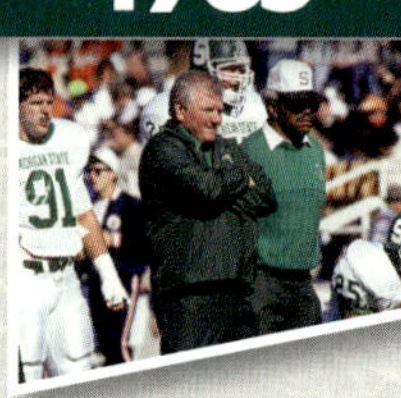

1988
Michigan State plays its first Rose Bowl game in 22 years on January 1.

1999
Spartans beat Notre Dame, Michigan, Ohio State, and Penn State for the first time since 1965.

Jim Crowley takes over as coach and leads the team to four straight winning seasons.

1929

Spartans compete in their first bowl game, playing in the Orange Bowl against Auburn January 1.

1938

Michigan State wins back-to-back national championships.

1951–52

Biggie Munn coaches the Spartans to a Rose Bowl victory against UCLA on January 1.

1954

The Coaches' Poll ranks Michigan State No. 1 in the nation.

1965

Michigan State shocks Notre Dame 34–31 with a field goal on September 18.

2010

Mark Dantonio guides Michigan State to its first Rose Bowl victory in 26 years on January 1.

2014

The Spartans edge Baylor 42–41 in the Cotton Bowl on New Year's Day.

2015

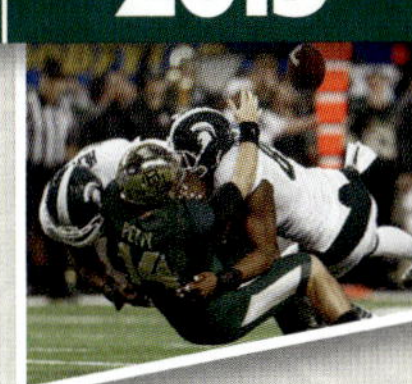

Michigan State earns a spot in the College Football Playoff but loses to eventual champion Alabama in the semifinals on New Year's Eve.

2015

Michigan State defeats Washington 42–17 in the Holiday Bowl for its fifth bowl victory in seven years.

2017

QUICK STATS

PROGRAM INFO*

Michigan Agricultural College Aggies, 1896–1935

Michigan State University Spartans, 1935–

NATIONAL CHAMPIONSHIPS

1951, 1952, 1955, 1957, 1965, and 1966

OTHER ACHIEVEMENTS

Big Ten championships: 9

Bowl appearances: 27

Bowl record: 12–15

KEY PLAYERS

(POSITION, SEASONS WITH TEAM)

Don Coleman (T, 1949–51)

Kirk Cousins (QB, 2008–11)

Darqueze Dennard (CB, 2010–13)

Greg Jones (LB, 2007–10)

Andre Rison (WR, 1985–88)

Charles Rogers (WR, 2001–02)

Bubba Smith (DE, 1964–66)

Percy Snow (LB, 1987–89)

George Webster (LB, 1964–66)

Lorenzo White (RB, 1984–87)

*statistics through 2017 season

KEY COACHES

Chester Brewer (1903–10, 1917, 1919)
58–23–7

Mark Dantonio (2007–)
100–45; 5–4 (bowl games)

Duffy Daugherty (1954–72)
109–69–5; 1–1(bowl games)

Clarence "Biggie" Munn (1947–53)
54–9–2; 1–0 (bowl games)

George Perles (1983–94)
68–67–4; 3–4 (bowl games)

HOME STADIUM

Spartan Stadium (1923–)

QUOTES & ANECDOTES

Michigan State's mascot Sparty is a muscular athlete in Spartan armor. Sparty won three national championships in four years at the Universal Cheer Association's competition.

"I'll tell you how you sum up the moment. You're going to be able to come back here and see Michigan State up there winning on that plaque outside this Rose Bowl 50 years from now with your grandchildren. That's what you're going to be able to do."—Coach Mark Dantonio after winning the 2014 Rose Bowl

Coach Clarence "Biggie" Munn guided Michigan State to a 28-game winning streak that spanned from the fourth game of 1950 to the fifth game of 1953, the longest unbeaten streak in program history.

"The difference between good and great is just a little extra effort."
—Biggie Munn

"I think it's amazing that 50 years later, we're celebrating a game that ended in a tie. The fact that it did end in a tie has caused it to preserve itself and its legacy over the years."—Jimmy Raye, the Spartans' quarterback who played in the 1966 "Game of the Century" tie with Notre Dame

GLOSSARY

All-American
Designation for players chosen as the best amateurs in the country in a particular sport.

athletic director
An administrator who oversees a university's athletics program.

conference
A group of schools that join together to create a league for their sports teams.

consensus
A consensus winner is when multiple polls agree.

draft
A system that allows teams to acquire new players coming into a league.

recruit
Convincing a high school player to attend a college, usually to play sports.

rival
An opponent with whom a player or team has a fierce and ongoing competition.

scholarship
Money awarded to students to pay for education expenses.

tenure
The holding of an office or position.

upset
An unexpected victory by a supposedly weaker team or player.

FOR MORE INFORMATION

ONLINE RESOURCES

To learn more about the Michigan State Spartans, visit abdobooklinks.com. These links are routinely monitored and updated to provide the most current information available

BOOKS

Ebling, Jack. *Heart of a Spartan: The Story of a Michigan State Football Renaissance.* Lansing, MI: Sports Community, 2012.

Emmerich, Michael. *100 Things Michigan State Fans Should Know & Do Before They Die.* Chicago, IL: Triumph Books, 2013.

Seibold, Jack. *Spartan Sports Encyclopedia: A History of the Michigan State Men's Athletic Program.* New York: Sports Publishing, 2014.

PLACE TO VISIT

Spartan Stadium
325 West Shaw Lane
East Lansing, MI 48824
517-355-1610
msuspartans.com/facilities/spartan-stadium.html

Spartan Stadium has been home to Michigan State football since 1923. The Spartans have won seventy percent of the more than five hundred games played there.

ABOUT THE AUTHOR

Todd Karpovich is an award-winning writer based in Baltimore, Maryland. He has written for ESPN.com, the Associated Press, MLB.com, Sports Xchange, the *Baltimore Sun*, and other national media outlets. He is the coauthor of *Skipper Supreme: Buck Showalter and the Baltimore Orioles.*